To **Holly**

For being good.
MERRY CHRISTMAS!

From

Each and every Christmas Eve's Eve (the day before Christmas Eve), Santa checked his list to see which boy or girl had been extra good. Whoever was at the top of the list would be invited to Lapland to meet all the reindeer, elves and of course Santa himself.

At the very top of his list was a little girl called HOLLY

HOLLY

Rudolph (the fastest of all the reindeer) flew straight to her house and popped her on his back.

Then quick as a flash they ZOOMed back to Lapland.

5

She had a **fantastic** day at Lapland, helping the elves prepare the presents for all the good boys and girls.

Early on Christmas Eve morning, Santa was about to get dressed when he realised something was wrong!

His bright red suit was GONE!

Santa looked in his wardrobe but it wasn't there.

Then he looked on the back of his door.

He even looked under his bed but his suit was nowhere to be found!

"Oh no, this is terrible!" exclaimed Santa. "I can't deliver Christmas presents without my suit on!"

7

A very red-faced and worried Santa called for Holly and the elves to come into the grotto's great hall to tell them the awful news that his suit was missing.

Santa then asked all his little helpers to try and find the suit or he would have to cancel Christmas!

Santa didn't want
to cancel Christmas.

So he tried on a
green elf suit
but it was
too small.

Then he tried on
Mrs Claus's dress
but it was too short.

Finally, he tried on
Rudolph's favourite blanket...
but it was too **big**,
too itchy and very smelly!

Santa didn't know **what** to do.

9

Holly and the elves looked all over Santa's Grotto. They looked in the toy-making room.

They looked in the kitchen.

Welcome to Santa's GROTTO

10

They looked in the
present-wrapping room.

They looked in Santa's workshop.

They even
looked in
the reindeer'
stinky stables.

But Santa's suit was nowhere to be found.

11

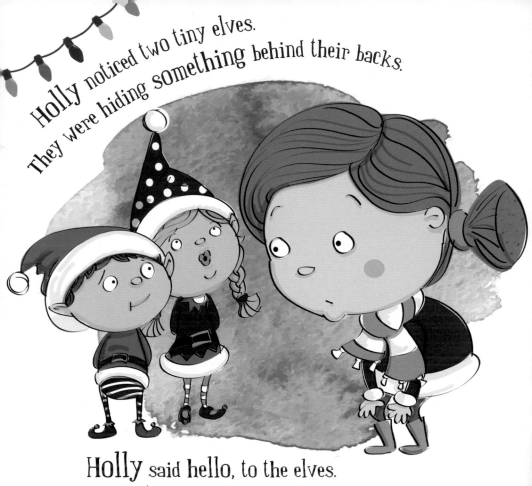

Holly noticed two tiny elves.
They were hiding something behind their backs.

Holly said hello, to the elves.
"What are you hiding behind your backs?"

The sorry-looking elves showed Holly
what they were hiding. It was Santa's bright red
suit but it was as tiny as a baby's bib!

The elves explained to Holly
that they had been trying to help Santa
by washing his suit but it had shrunk!
Now they didn't know what to do.

Suddenly
Holly
had a
FANTASTIC
idea!

Holly asked the
two elves to go and look for:
Some white tinsel.

Some black ribbon.

Some shiny
gold paper...

...and three different
coloured baubles.

Then bring them to Santa's workshop
as quickly as possible.

The elves found
everything on the
list and placed each
one on the
workshop table.

"Perfect!" said Holly as she pulled out a huge piece of red material and put it on the table.

"We're going to make Santa a brand new suit," she said.

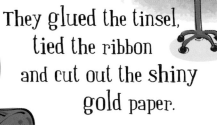

They glued the tinsel, tied the ribbon and cut out the shiny gold paper.

Then they sewed on the bright baubles.

Finally it was all finished... but had they made it in time?

15

A very nervous Santa looked at the big cuckoo clock on the wall.

It would soon be too late to start delivering the presents.

Santa was going to have to cancel Christmas!

16

Santa was taken aback as Holly
and her two helpers ran into the room
with his brand new, bright red suit.

It had a tinsel collar and cuffs.

A belt and buckle
made of shiny
gold paper...

...and three
beautiful baubles
as buttons.

18

Santa was very surprised and **extremely** happy.

He tried on his new suit.

It was PERFECT!

HO HO HO!

Santa was smiling again.

And so were all the elves, reindeer and Mrs Claus – because Christmas was back on!

"Thank you, you have saved Christmas!" exclaimed Santa, as he climbed into his sleigh to head off to deliver all the presents. "But where did you find the red fabric?"

Holly just smiled as she got ready to make her way home.

20